A Long Way to Go

About the ONCE UPON AMERICA™ Series

Who is affected by the events of history? Not only the famous and powerful. Individuals from every part of society contribute a *story*—and so weave together *history*. Some of the finest storytellers bring their talents to this series of historical fiction, based on careful research and designed specifically for readers ages 7–11. These are tales of young people growing up in a young, dynamic country. Each ONCE UPON AMERICA volume shapes the reader's understanding of the people who built America and of his or her own role in our unfolding history. For history is a story that we continue to write, with a chapter for each of us beginning, "Once upon America."

A Long Way to Go

BY ZIBBY ONEAL

ILLUSTRATED BY MICHAEL DOOLING

PUFFIN BOOKS

PUFFIN BOOKS
Published by the Penguin Group
Penguin Books USA Inc., 375 Hudson Street, New York, New York 10014, U.S.A.
Penguin Books Ltd, 27 Wrights Lane, London W8 5TZ, England
Penguin Books Australia Ltd, Ringwood, Victoria, Australia
Penguin Books Canada Ltd, 10 Alcorn Avenue, Toronto, Ontario, Canada M4V 3B2
Penguin Books (N.Z.) Ltd, 182–190 Wairau Road, Auckland 10, New Zealand

Penguin Books Ltd, Registered Offices: Harmondsworth, Middlesex, England

First published in the United States of America by Viking Penguin,
a division of Penguin Books USA Inc., 1990
Published in Puffin Books, 1992
10

ONCE UPON AMERICA™ is a trademark of Viking Penguin,
a division of Penguin Books USA Inc.

LIBRARY OF CONGRESS CATALOGING-IN-PUBLICATION DATA
Oneal, Zibby.
A long way to go / by Zibby Oneal; illustrated by Michael Dooling.
p.   cm.—(A Once upon America book)
Originally published: New York : Viking Penguin, 1990.
Summary: Eight-year-old Lila deals with the women's suffrage
movement that rages during World War I.
ISBN 0-14-032950-1
[1. Women—Suffrage—Fiction.   2. World War, 1914–1918—Fiction.]
I. Dooling, Michael, ill.   II. Title.   III. Series: Once upon America.
PZ7.0552Lo   1992   [Fic]—dc20   92-4628

Printed in the United States of America
Set in Goudy Old Style

To my mother, Mary Elizabeth Bisgard,
with love

Contents

A Long Way to Go

The Yellow Flower

Something was wrong. Lila felt it in her bones. Papa was home too early. Mama had shut the parlor doors. And she, Lila, ten years old, had been sent out to walk with her brother, George.

It was embarrassing to be out walking with her baby brother and his nursemaid. Lila hated it. She followed after Katie Rose and the baby carriage, dragging her feet.

Once around Gramercy Park they went, then around again. The trees were yellow in the warm September sunshine. A New York cab stopped down the street. Lila hardly noticed. Her eye was on the brown-stone house where something was wrong. What had happened? Why were Papa and Mama talking quietly in the closed parlor? And why had she been sent out to walk? It must have been the telegram, she thought. It had to be.

"What did it say?" she asked Katie Rose for the third time. "Tell me. What *did* it?"

Katie hesitated. She sighed. "Ah, just that your Grandma's in jail is all."

"What?" Lila stopped.

"She got arrested with those suffering ladies."

"Suffrage," said Lila.

"Well, them. Those ladies that want to vote. They got arrested picketing the White House."

So that was why Grandmama had gone down to Washington! Lila nodded. Grandmama was a suffragist. She gave speeches. She marched in parades. She was doing anything she could, she said, to try to change the law so that women could vote. "It's a scandal that women can't vote," she said. "This is 1917, not the Dark Ages." But now she was in jail.

Lila looked down at her high-button shoes, at her long, scratchy stockings that were wrinkled at the knees, at the shadow of her hair bow like a big butterfly on the sidewalk. "What's picketing?" she asked.

"Carrying signs. Bothering people," said Katie Rose.

"Who was she bothering?"

Katie sniffed. "The president, that's who! I call it

wrong bothering the president when there's a war on."

"Pooh," said Lila. Katie always talked that way. Now that her sweetheart had gone off to fight the Germans in France she didn't talk about much *but* the war.

Of course Lila knew that the war was important. It was because of the war that Mama knitted socks for soldiers and rolled gauze into bandages every Tuesday at the Red Cross. It was because of the war that Papa swore at the headlines in the paper and bought Liberty Bonds. Of course it was important, but this was something else. This was Grandmama! Katie didn't seem to understand.

All afternoon Lila worried. Had her grandmother done something terribly wrong? Would they keep her in jail for years? There was no one to ask but Katie Rose and she didn't know the answers.

Lila worried all through supper which she always ate in the nursery with Katie Rose and George. When Mama came up to say good-night, Lila hugged her neck and whispered, "When will Grandmama come home?" But Mama only shook her head and said that little girls shouldn't worry about grown-up matters.

Lila stared into the darkness. She imagined jail cells and handcuffs and tin plates of dry bread. She imagined Grandmama growing thin and pale. Her eyes filled with tears. Lila loved her grandmother very much. She couldn't believe she'd do anything wrong.

Lila began to grow sleepy. Her eyes had almost

closed when she heard voices. At once she was wide awake. She crept to the top of the stairs and leaned over the banister. There, in the front hall, stood Grandmama taking off her hat. And there stood Papa in his vest and shirtsleeves.

"How could you do it?" Papa exclaimed.

"I might ask the same question." Grandmama replaced the pin in her hat and looked at Papa. "What were you thinking of, bailing me out of jail? I was there for a purpose."

"I won't have my own mother breaking the law and making a spectacle of herself."

Grandmama gave him a long look. Lila was leaning so far over the banister that she was almost upside down.

"There's no law saying a person can't picket that I'm aware of," said Grandmama.

"But picketing the White House in wartime!"

"Well, we've tried everything else. We've asked the Congress for an amendment to the Constitution. We've asked President Wilson many times as well. It seems that no one in the government thinks that women should vote."

"No wonder," Papa said. "As anyone knows, a woman's place is at home, not in politics."

"Fiddlesticks!"

"If women start behaving like men, what's going to happen to children? What's going to happen to the home?"

"Not much, I imagine."

Grandmama was patting her white hair smooth. Papa was red in the face.

"*I* vote for the members of this family," he said.

Grandmama snorted. "I can remember when you couldn't even talk."

Lila couldn't help giggling at that. Fist stuffed against her mouth, she tried not to, but her giggles leaked out. Papa and Grandmama looked up. "Lila!" Papa thundered.

"Oh, my sakes," said Grandmama. "It won't hurt Lila to hear this. She'll be a woman herself one day."

But then Grandmama looked suddenly very, very serious. "Can't you understand what this means to us, Harry? There are women all over this country working to be treated as equal citizens. After all, this is a democracy—so they say."

Lila decided she had better not wait to hear more, noticing the way that her papa was frowning. In bed, she pulled up the covers to her chin and waited for Grandmama to come tell her good-night. After a while, the door opened a crack and Grandmama slipped in. She sat down beside Lila and stroked her hair. "I brought you something from Washington," she said, and put a flower down on Lila's pillow. It smelled strong and spicy. Lila touched it.

"It's a yellow chrysanthemum," said Grandmama. "The suffragists wear them. Yellow's our color."

Lila touched the flower's cool petals. "I can wear it to school," she said.

Grandmama nodded and kept talking softly. "By the time you're grown, women will be voting. That's what the yellow chrysanthemum means—that the Constitution will be changed. And we'll do it if I have to go to jail ten more times."

"Oh, don't go to jail again," said Lila, but her neck prickled with excitement as she said it. Going to jail seemed such a daring thing to do.

Rules

In the morning, the flower was half-wilted. At break-fast, Mama said Lila couldn't wear it to school.

"But I want to wear it," Lila said. "I don't care if it's a little wilted." And then she swallowed, remembering that she wasn't allowed to talk back.

"Papa wouldn't approve of the flower. I think you had better leave it at home."

And so the flower stayed home in a glass of water, and Lila started off to school. It was the beginning of a horrible day.

"Your grandma's a convict," Billy Ash said the moment Lila walked into her classroom.

"She isn't," said Lila, backing up against the blackboard.

"Yes, she is. My father read it in the paper. She's in jail."

"She isn't. She's home."

"She got arrested outside the White House!" Billy said it so loudly that everyone in the room heard. "They took her to jail in a police wagon!"

This was true. Lila couldn't deny it. Grandmama had told her all about it at breakfast. "But she wasn't doing anything wrong. She was just standing there holding a sign asking the president to let women vote."

"Why'd they arrest her then?"

"They said the suffragists were holding up traffic, but they weren't. It was all the people watching them who were doing that."

"That's not what the paper said. It said there was almost a riot. People were tearing down the signs and flags and spitting at the women."

Lila felt confused. Grandmama hadn't mentioned that. "Well, anyway," she said, "my grandmother saw the president. He tipped his hat to her."

"Oh, go on."

"He did." Lila stood straight and her voice grew louder. "While the women were standing there with their banners, his car drove out through the gate and he tipped his hat to them."

Billy didn't say anything. Neither did anyone else. Then Lila spoke up, "My grandmother says at least he's polite even if he doesn't want women to vote."

"Women are too weak to vote," Billy said. "Weak in the head, I mean."

Lila stuck out her chin. "You wait and see."

"I guess I'll wait till butter flies."

"I guess you won't," said Lila. And then Miss Irvin came into the room and nobody could say anything.

All through penmanship, Lila thought about Grandmama. She practiced making perfect *R*s spaced evenly between her paper's ruled lines. She tried to imagine anyone daring to spit at Grandmama. In geography, tracing a map of the Belgian Congo, she thought of her flower at home.

If she were wearing the flower in her hair, everyone would know that she was for women voting. But was she? She wasn't sure. Why wasn't Papa? Why wasn't Mama? Why wasn't the president of the United States? Lila put down her pencil and looked out the window. Why was Grandmama different? Lila didn't know what to think. All she knew was that she didn't like Billy Ash saying she was weak in the head.

On the way home from school, Lila felt tired. Billy Ash wasn't the only one who mentioned Grandmama that day. Margaret Stevens had said it was rude to picket. Alice Palmer had said her mother was shocked. Lila had tried hard to speak up for Grandmama, but she was running out of energy.

At the corner of Twenty-first Street, she stopped while a vegetable wagon passed. The old horse drawing the wagon snorted. Tomatoes and peppers and corn lay gleaming on a bed of melting ice. Lila had seen children follow after the wagon, grabbing for ice shavings, but she had never done it herself. It was one of the things she was not allowed to do, even when the wagon stopped at her own house to sell vegetables.

A motorcar honked. The wagon rolled on. Lila started down the next block between brownstone houses like her own, each with steep front steps and a shiny brass knocker on the door. She sighed. There were so many things she was not allowed to do: talk too loudly, interrupt, ask too many questions, show off. She could not roll down her stockings even on hot days, get grass stains on her dresses playing in the park, turn cartwheels. It all had to do with being a girl, she thought. Who cared if boys turned cartwheels?

Lila felt gloomy. Girls couldn't do much of anything fun, and besides that they couldn't vote. And then she stopped still. An awful thought suddenly occurred to her. Someday her dumb little brother George would be able to vote just because he was a boy. He'd go off voting and she'd sit at home unless the law changed. This was too much for Lila. With her toe she kicked the sidewalk hard. Then she remembered that she was not allowed to scuff her shoes, so she kicked it even harder.

Grandmama was in the front hall putting on her hat when Lila came in. "Where are you going?" Lila said.

14

"Out speaking."

Lila nodded. In the afternoons, Grandmama often went out to speak. Lila had heard her practice. "What are you going to talk about today?" she asked.

"Today I'm going to speak about the state election coming up. I'm going to ask the men of New York to give women a vote in this state even if the United States Congress won't give them a vote in this country. It's really a pretty good speech." She smiled. "Just think, Lila, all over New York there are women like me speaking on street corners every day. I believe we're bound to win, don't you?"

Lila nodded, leaning against the hall table, watching Grandmama put on her gloves. "*Why* doesn't Papa want women to vote?" she said.

"You heard him. He thinks women should stay at home and mind their own business. He doesn't think that what goes on in this country is our business."

"Isn't it?"

"Of course it is."

"Then why doesn't Mama want to vote?"

Grandmama looked thoughtful. "I guess she thinks it's her duty to agree with your father. There are a lot of women who think that way."

"Not you."

Grandmama laughed. "Not me. I think women have a right to help make the laws they live with."

Lila looked down at the scuffed toe of her shoe and said suddenly, "Can I come with you?"

"I wish you could." And Lila knew what she wasn't

saying—that Lila couldn't because Papa wouldn't approve.

Face pressed against the parlor window, Lila watched Grandmama start up the street, walking quickly, carrying the wooden box she stood on when she spoke. Lila thought she looked like a queen.

In the fenced-in park across the street, two little girls were rolling hoops along the walk. Three more sat on the grass playing with dolls. Lila could see Katie Rose sitting on a bench with the other nursemaids. They reminded her of animals in the zoo, all of them there behind the bars of the tall iron fence.

Lila sat down on the piano stool and whirled around. She wished she could put a record on the Victrola, at least. But she wasn't allowed. Only Papa did that.

Lila sighed. She felt like an animal in the zoo herself. There was such a lot she was never allowed to do.

Jawbreakers and Penny Candy

Katie Rose had Saturdays off. On that day, right after lunch, she went home to help her mother. Sometime, she promised, she'd take Lila along, and one Saturday in September that happened.

First thing in the morning, while she was brushing Lila's hair, Katie Rose said, "How would you like to go home with me today?"

Lila forgot how the brush was pulling her long hair. "Really? Today?" she said.

"I asked your mama and she agreed, if we are sure

to be home by supper." All morning Lila squirmed with excitement.

Soon after lunch they set off, Katie Rose prim and pretty in her Saturday hat, and Lila wearing her best coat with the beaver collar. They walked to Fourth Avenue and waited for the trolley. Lila had her fare in her pocket.

"You mustn't expect anything grand," Katie said when they were sitting side by side on the trolley's slippery wooden seat. "We're poor and that's a fact. We all have to help. Delia and Sheila help Mama with her sewing from the shirtwaist factory. Mike sells papers and Annie watches the babies."

Lila nodded. Katie Rose had told her many times about her brothers and sisters, but sometimes Lila got mixed up. There were so many of them.

The trolley rattled along Fourth Avenue, sometimes ringing its bell. Lila looked out the windows to left and right. They rode past rows of shops with striped awnings, past a hotel where a doorman stood holding packages, past a square where fountains were spraying, on and on, starting and stopping. Then the buildings began to look shabbier and the sidewalks became more crowded. Finally Katie stood up. "Next stop's ours." They made their way to the front of the car as the trolley slowed, and climbed down the steep steps when it stopped.

Suddenly they were in a crowd of people. Lila had never seen so many people. "Come along then," Katie

Rose said. "It's a bit of a walk from here." She took Lila's hand.

Lila hurried to keep up, trying to look about her as she went. It was like stumbling into a festival or fair. The curbs were lined with pushcarts loaded with every kind of thing for sale—shoelaces and suspenders, bags of potatoes, piles of apples, pillows, pots and pans, barrels of fish. There were huge tin cans full of milk, mounds of shoes, heaps of long underwear. Lila stared. Children were playing in the street, dodging trucks and delivery wagons. Scrawny cats darted under the wheels of carts. Lila had never seen so much going on all at once.

She looked at the tenement buildings along the street and at the fire escapes where laundry was hanging, underwear in plain sight. A woman shook a mop from a window. There was a smell of cooking in the air. The street rang with shouts and laughter. It seemed to Lila that she had never been so far away from home before.

Katie Rose led her across the street toward a dull red building like the others. "Ah, there's Annie," she cried, and Lila saw a girl about her own age on the steps outside the building. She was holding a baby in her arms and watching another, bigger one. "My baby brothers," Katie said as they crossed the street.

Annie lifted the smallest baby onto her shoulder when she saw them coming. She smiled shyly at Lila. "I was hoping Katie Rose would bring you sometime."

Together they went into the building's dark hallway. They climbed a flight of steps and then another. On the third landing, Katie Rose pushed open a door and called, "I'm home! I brought Lila!"

A strong smell of cooking greeted Lila's nose. She blinked, coming in from the darkness of the hallway. In the center of the room was a table where two little girls were sitting with a woman who, Lila guessed, was Katie's mother. All of them were doing something that looked like sewing. "Pulling bastings, are you?" asked Katie Rose. "I told you, Lila, Sheila and Delia help Mama with her sewing. They pull basting threads. And that's Mike over there in the corner."

Before Lila had them sorted out, she was sitting at the table with them, drinking tea. The babies crawled around the legs of the chairs, and the rest of them laughed and told stories. Lila sipped her tea slowly and listened.

"Mike's going to take you out to see the sights, Lila," Katie Rose's mother said.

Lila looked up from her cup. She could see that he didn't want to. "Why doesn't Annie do it?" he muttered.

"You know very well why," said Annie.

"You don't have to take me," Lila said as she followed Mike back down the dark stairway.

"Naw, it's all right." But it didn't sound to Lila as if he really thought so.

"Why couldn't Annie?"

"She's got the babies to mind."

"Can't your mother and Katie do that?"

"Naw, it wouldn't be fair. Mama likes to sit a bit with Katie when she has a chance. Anyway, it's Annie's job, minding them."

"All the time?"

Mike pushed open the outside door and turned to look at her curiously. "After school and weekends," he said, as if he thought anyone would know that.

They stood on the sidewalk in the sunshine. "What d'you want to see?" Mike asked.

"I don't know what there is to see."

"You ever been to the flickers?"

"The what?"

"The motion picture show."

Lila shook her head. Of course she hadn't. Nice people didn't go to places like that, Mama said.

"Want to see one? It costs a nickel."

Lila fingered the change in her pocket. She could feel the smooth edge of a nickel there. All the while she was thinking she shouldn't go, her feet were following Mike down the street.

"Bet you've never seen a nickelodeon," he said. "They're swell. I go there all the time. We could go see a live show. They're swell, too, but they cost more."

The nickelodeon was enough for Lila. At the booth outside the door they paid. Then they went in and found chairs in the darkness. A prickle of excitement ran down Lila's spine as a gray, flickering picture appeared on the screen. Suddenly a train came rushing into view. A cowboy followed on a galloping horse. He waved a gun. The audience yelled. The train went hurtling off a cliff. The audience whistled and stamped on the floor. Then, all at once, nothing. The screen went blank. "Busted," Mike said. "It always happens. But don't worry. You get three reels for a nickel."

Soon the screen flickered again and a picture appeared. A bandit this time. Another chase. Lila stared. She sat without moving until the third reel ended and the lights came on, until Mike said, "It's over."

On the street she stood dazzled by daylight, waiting for whatever would happen next. "I bet you've never been to a penny candy store either," Mike said.

"I haven't."

She had never even imagined one, and she couldn't believe her eyes. In the long glass cases that ran the length of the store, there were gumdrops and jelly beans, jawbreakers, mounds of chocolate-covered cherries, peanuts, and long, thin licorice whips. They walked the whole length of the counter, inspecting the candy, running their fingers along the glass. "Anything costs a penny," Mike said, "but jawbreakers last longest."

Lila felt for pennies in her pocket. She had two, and so she chose a red jawbreaker for herself. Then she chose a green one for Annie because it didn't seem fair that Annie couldn't come.

Mouths full of candy, they wandered out the door. The street was busy as ever, but the slant of the sun had changed. Suddenly Mike's face was serious. "It's time to go get my papers," he said. "I mean the newspapers I sell. It's my job."

"Oh." Lila looked around her, at the alley where a baseball game was going on, at the bunch of boys pitching pennies on the sidewalk, at the horse-drawn ice wagon coming down the street. She sniffed the warm odor of sugar floating through the candy store door. She had never been any place that was so exciting. But now it was about to end. Mike was going off to sell his papers. Soon she and Katie Rose would take the trolley home and she would have supper in the nursery and play next day in the fenced-in park and remember not to dirty her dress.

"You better go stay with Annie now," Mike said. "I'll show you the way."

But she didn't want to go back. She didn't want it all to end. "Can't I come with you?"

"Naw, girls can't."

"Why can't they?"

"Girls don't sell papers."

"Why not?"

"They're too weak." Mike pretended to be holding up the hem of a skirt. "They're too del-i-cate."

Lila stuck out her chin. "I'm not."

"Sure you are. All girls are." He looked at her and grinned.

Lila didn't plan what happened next. It just seemed to happen. One minute Mike was grinning at her, and the next he was holding his jaw.

"What'd you hit me for?" he asked.

"Because of what you said." Or maybe because of what Billy Ash had said in school, or what Papa had said to Grandmama. Lila didn't know. Maybe she had hit him to show him she wasn't weak.

"What did I say?" He looked puzzled.

"That girls are weak and delicate."

"But it's true." She could see that he really believed it was true, that he hadn't meant to insult her. She didn't care. She was tired of hearing things like that.

"I could sell papers as well as you," she said. "Any girl could."

"You couldn't even carry them."

"I could!"

Mike was stroking his jaw as if it still hurt him. He looked at her. "Yeah?" he said. "Well, come on and try then."

Headlines

Lila counted more than thirty newsboys waiting to pick up their papers outside the office building where she and Mike stopped. A man was dumping great rope-bound bundles onto the sidewalk. "You wait here," Mike said and hurried into the crowd. In his cloth cap and knickers he looked just like every other boy waiting there. Lila soon lost sight of him.

She stood on the sidewalk, feeling out of place in her Sunday coat and white hair bow—the only girl on the street. Maybe this is a mistake, she thought. But then she thought again. She remembered the yellow chrysanthemum pressed in a book in her room at home. She remembered Grandmama striding off so proudly to speak. Of course she could sell papers!

In a few minutes, Mike was back, carrying a canvas bag on his shoulder. "Go ahead, take some," he said, "since you're so strong." He handed Lila the bag, half full.

Her shoulder sagged under the weight. "Heavy, aren't they?" Mike said.

Lila shrugged. "Not very."

She didn't think that he believed her. "Come on, then. I sell on the corner of Tenth Street," he said.

Lila tried to hurry. The strap of the bag cut into her shoulder, and the weight of it bumped against her hip, but she didn't intend to let that slow her down. She walked as fast as she could.

"The headlines aren't much good today," Mike said. "What I like is when there's a murder or the Germans torpedo a ship. That's when you really sell papers. All we got today is some speech about Liberty Bonds and a fire in a warehouse in Brooklyn." He shrugged. "So I'll have to use my imagination. That's what you do when the headlines aren't much. It's like advertising. Nobody's going to want to read the bond speech, of course, so I guess I'll have to work on the fire."

Lila didn't see how he could talk so much carrying papers. She could hardly breathe. Her shoulder ached and her arm was going numb. But of course she didn't say so. She wouldn't say so if she had to walk another five miles. She bit her lip and kept going.

Then, just when she thought she couldn't carry the papers much longer, when her arm felt dead as a stick of wood, they stopped. "This is it," said Mike. "My corner." He dropped most of his papers onto the sidewalk. Gratefully Lila dropped hers.

"Now let's see you sell," Mike said, but he didn't wait to watch. Instead he began running after customers, waving papers, shouting, "Read all about the big fire in Brooklyn! Read about the flames forty feet high!"

Lila pulled a paper from the bag and looked at it. She couldn't see where he was getting all that. The paper didn't say a thing about flames. It didn't really say much about the fire. That was what he meant by imagination, she guessed, but it didn't seem quite fair to fool people that way.

She ran her eyes down the front page. The bond speech. The fire. But then she saw, down at the bottom of the page, not taking much space, a small article headed, SUFFRAGISTS REFUSE TO EAT. Lila read as fast as she could. There were suffragists in jail in Washington who wouldn't eat a bite. They said they'd rather starve than do without the vote. The paper called it a hunger strike.

Lila's eyes widened. This was news. This was something interesting. And, besides, it was true. She pulled a few more papers from her bag and stood herself right

in the middle of the sidewalk. "Suffragists starving to death!" she yelled. "Read all about it!"

To her amazement, someone stopped to buy a paper. She tried again. "Read all about the ladies starving to death in Washington!" And, again, someone stopped.

"Crazy women," the man said, but he paid her and didn't seem to think it was strange at all to see a girl selling papers.

Lila felt encouraged. Over and over she waved her papers at people walking past. She shouted her headline until she was hoarse, but it felt good to be hoarse, to be shouting and running.

"President making women starve!" she cried. "They won't eat till they get to vote!" Anything she said seemed to work. People bought papers. Maybe they would have bought them anyway, thought Lila. She didn't know, but she didn't care. She was too busy selling. In no time, her bag was empty.

She hadn't had time to think about Mike, but now, bag empty, she turned around to look for him. He was leaning against a lamppost, watching her. "I sold them all," she said breathlessly.

"I noticed."

"Here's the money." She fished the change and a few bills from her pocket.

"You keep it."

"No. Why?"

"You earned it."

"But I didn't do it for that." Lila thought of Annie,

minding the babies, of the little girls pulling basting threads all afternoon. "You take the money. I just did it to show you I could."

"Yeah. Well." Mike kicked the lamppost with the toe of his shoe. "I guess you showed me."

There were things that Lila felt like saying, but she decided not to say them. Instead she picked up the empty canvas bag and slung it over her shoulder. Together they started back the way they had come.

It was twilight. The streets were filled with the sounds of horns and engines. Lights blossomed in shop windows. People hurried along the sidewalk. On a corner, leaning against the side of a parked truck, a man was playing a harmonica. "Over There," he played slowly, making the notes sound like a sleepy bugle call. "Over There." It was a tune Katie Rose sometimes sang when she was folding laundry, thinking about her sweetheart overseas. The music sounded soft and sad in the twilight.

The two of them walked on in silence, and the mournful notes of the harmonica followed after them. Lila felt too tired to talk. Her head swam with new things to think about—the candy store with all its treasures, the nickelodeon with its flickering screen, the pushcarts loaded with things to sell, the sounds and smells of this new neighborhood. But most of all it was selling papers that she wanted to remember— running after customers, yelling her headlines. The canvas bag swung against her shoulder. She smiled.

The men who sold goods from the pushcarts were packing up when the two of them turned the corner onto Mike's street. Lila could see Katie Rose standing on the steps at the end of the block, and she knew they should hurry, but instead she slowed down.

"I'm sorry I hit you," she said.

"Yeah, well, I'm sorry for what I said about girls."

"You just didn't know any better."

"I never saw a girl selling papers before." Then he turned to look at her and Lila thought that he looked shy. "You were good at it," he said. "You knew what to do."

Lila smiled and handed him the canvas bag and they went on down the street.

So now it was really over—the wonderful afternoon. Now she would go home with Katie Rose and turn into a proper little girl again. It was like the end of a fairy tale, Lila thought. Except it was sad.

On the trolley she leaned against Katie Rose and closed her eyes. It was over, Lila thought, but she would remember, and a memory, like a jawbreaker, lasted a long, long time.

The Speech

"And then," said Lila on Sunday morning, bouncing on Grandmama's bed. "And then—"

"And then Katie Rose brought you home."

"Yes."

"Lila, you've told me all about it three times."

She had. She couldn't help it. Saturday afternoon was like a story she didn't want to finish, like a book of beautiful colored pictures that she couldn't bear to close.

"Oh, I liked it all so much, but I'm not going to tell anyone else about it. Just you." Lila looked out the window at the sunlight on the fence around the park. "I wish girls could sell papers," she said a little sadly. "I mean all the time."

"There are more and more things that girls can do. Think of all the jobs women have now that there's a war on. When I was your age we didn't dream of working in offices and factories."

"That's women. I mean girls." And then, "Do you think that if women could vote, they'd let girls sell papers?"

Grandmama laughed. "I don't know. I suppose there'd be a better chance of that happening."

"Then I'm a suffragist," Lila said. "I *thought* I was, but now I'm sure."

"That's fine."

Lila frowned. "But what can I do?"

"Believe that women have rights the same as men."

That wasn't what Lila had in mind. She wanted action. She wanted to shout headlines, run around yelling. "I could give speeches," she said. She imagined herself standing on a wooden box speaking to crowds in the street. It would be a lot like selling papers.

But Grandmama only laughed again. "You're still too young to make speeches."

"But I want to do *something*. It's no use just sitting around believing things."

Grandmama looked thoughtful. "Well, there's a suffragist parade a week or so before the state election. We're going to march up Fifth Avenue all the way from Washington Square to Fifty-ninth Street."

"With signs?" said Lila. "And banners?"

"Oh, yes, and music, too. We're going to make people notice us."

"Would you take me?"

"Well, I was thinking—"

Lila sat up straight. "I'm coming."

"But not without permission you aren't. Not unless your mama and papa agree."

"I'll make them agree," said Lila, though she had no idea how she'd do that.

"Well, I'll try to help you," Grandmama said. "At least I'll mention the parade."

Lila sat quietly in church with her hands in her lap. She played nicely with George until lunchtime, rolling his ball to him over and over though this was the most boring game in the world. She sat straight at the table and ate all her lunch, though that included beets. Really, Lila thought, she was being so perfect it was hard to see how Mama and Papa could say no.

But that was what Papa said. While they were waiting for dessert, Grandmama brought up the parade. She did it in a kind of offhanded way, as if it were something she'd only just remembered. "And I think Lila would like to march, too," she said. Lila looked down at her napkin and crossed her fingers. But Papa said no.

It was such a small word, no, but it seemed to Lila that it was the biggest word in her life. So many nos.

She felt tears of disappointment prickling in her eyes. She couldn't look up.

When, after lunch, Papa said, "Come on, Lila, it's time for our Sunday walk," Lila felt like saying, "No!" She didn't want to go for a walk with her father. She felt too mad and disappointed. All the same, she went to get her coat, because a little girl didn't say no to her father.

"Which way shall we walk?" he asked her when they were standing on the pavement.

"I don't care." And she didn't. She didn't care at all.

"What about Fifth Avenue then?"

Lila had known he'd choose that. Papa liked walking along Fifth Avenue, looking at the new motorcars pass by. One day, he said, he thought he might buy one.

And so they walked over to Fifth Avenue. Lila was wearing her best coat again and clean white gloves because Papa liked her to look like a lady when they went walking. But her hands felt crowded in the gloves and her shoulders felt crowded in her coat. She felt crowded all over.

At the corner of Fifth Avenue, they turned and walked north, past banks and office buildings, past shops and department stores. Usually Lila liked looking into the department store windows, but today they didn't seem exciting. She thought of the pushcarts on Katie Rose's street. Fifth Avenue was dull.

"Has the cat got your tongue?" Papa said.

"No. I'm thinking."

"About important things?"

"I was thinking about the parade. It's going to come right up this street."

"Lila, you must forget the parade."

But how could she? She couldn't stop thinking about it, even though the thinking made her sad.

They waited to cross the street while a car passed. "That's a Pierce Arrow," Papa said. "It's really something, isn't it?"

Lila nodded. She supposed so.

"Maybe when George is older we'll buy one like that. He can learn to drive it."

"What about me?"

"Oh, you'll be a beautiful grown lady by then. You can ride in the back and tell George where to take you. You'll have all kinds of pretty clothes to wear. We'll go shopping for things like the dress in that window."

Lila glanced at the dress in the shop window. She had to admit it was pretty. She wondered why she didn't like it more, and then she knew. It looked like the kind of dress that was for sitting around doing nothing.

"I'd rather learn how to drive a motorcar," she said. "I'd rather be *doing* something."

Papa didn't understand. "There'll be plenty for you to do. Tea dances and parties and all that sort of thing."

"Those aren't the things I want to do."

"No? What then?"

"Oh!" Lists of things came tumbling into Lila's head. She wanted to march in the parade, turn cartwheels, walk on her hands, roll her stockings down. She wanted to run and yell, sell papers—but that was not what Papa meant. He meant later, when she was grown-up. What did she want to do *then?* Lila closed her eyes and squeezed them tight. "I want to vote," she said.

The words were out before she knew she was going to say them, but suddenly they seemed just right. "I want to be able to vote same as George."

When she opened her eyes, Papa was looking at her. "That's what you want more than anything?"

Lila nodded. She dug her fists into her pockets and looked up at Papa bravely. "It's what Grandmama says. Girls are people, too. They have rights. It isn't fair the way it is. Billy Ash says he's smarter than me just because he's a boy. But I'm the one who gets all A's, not him. So why should he be allowed to vote and not me? Why should George if I can't? It's not fair, Papa. It's not fair to girls."

Lila paused for breath, but she couldn't stop talking. "When I grow up, I want to be just like Grandmama. I want to make things fair for everyone. That's why I want to march in the parade—to show people that's what I think. And if they put me in jail for marching, then I just won't eat, like the ladies in Washington."

Then Lila stopped. She didn't have anything else to say.

"Well," said Papa, "that was quite a speech."

Lila couldn't tell what he was thinking. His face was very serious. She wondered if he would stop loving her now because of all she'd said. She wondered if he'd already stopped. She waited for him to say something more, but he said nothing at all. He took her hand and they went on walking.

Lila's feet slapped along beside him. It was too late now to take it back, and, anyway, she couldn't take it back without lying. She'd said what she meant. But Papa wasn't saying anything at all. He was looking straight ahead as if he had forgotten all about her, as if he didn't know she was there any more.

Lila felt hollow in the middle. She bit the insides of her cheeks to keep from crying. On the way home, she counted cracks in the sidewalk.

When they reached the corner of Twenty-first Street and were almost home, Papa said, "How did you happen to know about those women in Washington, the ones who aren't eating? Did Grandmama tell you?"

Lila shook her head, still counting cracks. "No," she said. "I read it in the paper."

"Did you really? For heaven's sake." Lila could have sworn, if she hadn't known better, that he sounded proud of her.

After supper, she had her bath and watched Katie Rose laying out her clothes for school the next day. The same old stockings. The same old dress. Lila sighed. Everything was the same old thing again, except that now it would be different with Papa. She climbed out of the tub and wrapped herself in a towel. She went into her room to put on her nightgown.

And that was when Grandmama came in. She had a funny, puzzled sort of expression. "It looks as if we'll be going to the parade together," she said.

Lila paused. The damp ends of her hair swung against her shoulders. "What?"

"Your father says you may go."

"With you? To the parade?" Lila felt as if she couldn't take it all in so fast.

"That's what he says."

"But why?"

Grandmama shrugged. "I don't know what you said to him on that walk, but you must have said something."

Lila swallowed. He had called it a speech. She had made a speech and he'd listened! A bubble of happiness began to rise inside her. He had listened and it was all right. She grinned at Grandmama. She dropped her towel. And then right there, in the middle of her bedroom, stark naked, she turned a cartwheel.

The Parade

There were weeks of waiting before the parade. October crawled by like a snail. Lila imagined marching a hundred times before, at last, the day arrived, the special Saturday.

She woke in a shiver of excitement. She could hardly hold still while Katie Rose braided her hair. "You button your shoes yourself," Katie Rose said. "I can't manage with so much wiggling." And she handed Lila the buttonhook.

"Will you be sure to remember to tell Mike that I'm marching?"

Katie Rose snorted. "Do you think I could forget? You remind me every day."

Lila laughed. She was hoping that maybe—just maybe—Mike would come out to watch the parade.

"And tell Annie I wish she could march, too," Lila said. "Tell her I'm marching for her."

And then she jumped up and started downstairs because she couldn't hold still for more than a minute.

Grandmama was in the parlor, reading the paper. "I'm ready!" Lila cried.

Grandmama looked up. "That's fine, but you'll have a bit of a wait. The parade won't begin for several hours."

Lila twirled on the piano stool. She practiced marching between the parlor windows. Grandmama rattled the paper. "President Wilson has come to his senses, I see. He says he wishes our cause godspeed."

"What does that mean?" asked Lila.

"It means he wishes us luck. He's changing his spots, I think, just like your papa."

"What does *that* mean?"

"He's changing his mind. It says here he's leaning toward a constitutional amendment."

"So maybe there won't *be* a parade?"

"Of course there'll be a parade. We haven't *got* the amendment yet."

Lila let out her breath, relieved. She wondered how to spend the next few hours.

When at last they set out for the parade, Mama

stood in the parlor window, waving. Lila skipped and whirled up the sidewalk. They were going to catch a cab at the corner.

The cab dropped them a block from Washington Square. Lila could hear snatches of music as they walked toward it. "Those are the bands warming up," Grandmama said. "There's going to be a lot of music."

Lila trotted along beside her. The music grew louder and louder. And then they were in Washington Square, and Lila's eyes opened round as saucers.

There were women everywhere, hundreds and hundreds of them. Some carried flags, some were unrolling banners with words printed on them. There were women dressed in nurses' uniforms, women in Red Cross costumes, women wearing yellow chrysanthemums in their hats. So many women! There were old women, young women, white women, black women. There was even a woman standing in line propped on crutches.

"How can she march on crutches?" Lila whispered.

"She can if she makes her mind up to do it," Grandmama said. "That's what this is all about."

"Line up! Line up!" someone was shouting. A bass drum boomed. Grandmama took Lila's hand and they slipped quickly into line.

And then the music began. All at once, all the bands were playing and the columns of women began to move. Left, left. Lila was marching. Above her, the yellow banners streamed.

Out of Washington Square they marched and onto Fifth Avenue. Before and behind came the sound of the drums, and the flags snapped in the breeze. Left, left. On they went up the street, marching in time to the music.

From the curbs came the sound of whistles and cheers. Yellow streamers flew from the shop doors. White-gloved policemen held back the crowds as the bands and the marchers passed.

Lila felt she could march forever, her feet in step with the drums. Back straight, chin up. Left, left, left.

Just as they were crossing Tenth Street, it happened. The bands were playing "Over There." People on the sidewalk were shouting. Lila was looking into the crowd—just in case maybe—when something splashed at her feet.

It splashed and then it splattered red pulp and yellow seeds all over her stockings, all over the hem of her coat. "Someone threw a tomato!" she cried. "Someone threw it right at me!" She tugged Grandmama's hand. There were tears in her eyes.

Grandmama looked down. "Never mind. Just keep marching."

"But, Grandmama, a tomato! It's all over my legs!"

"These things happen sometimes, Lila. It is part of doing what we're doing. There are lots of people who don't want us to vote, lots who don't like this parade. Now be a brave girl. Show them they can't stop you. Keep marching."

Lila thought she was going to cry. Her feet kept moving, but she had lost step. She looked down at the red juice all over her white stockings. And then she got mad. She stuck out her chin and looked straight ahead, and her feet began to move in time with the music.

Left, left. A tomato couldn't stop her. She thought about the woman on crutches. She thought of the women who were still in jail in Washington and about the ones who weren't eating. She thought of all the speeches that Grandmama had made. She thought of her own speech to Papa. She remembered Annie minding the babies and Sheila and Delia pulling bastings all day Saturday. A tomato wasn't much, she thought. A tomato was nothing.

Head up, looking straight ahead, Lila marched on, her feet keeping time with the music.

By the time the parade reached Twenty-first Street, Lila's stockings were dry. The bands were playing "Tipperary." Lila knew the words to that song. She knew they talked about a long way to go. She began to sing to herself as she marched along.

And then Grandmama began singing. And soon women all around them had taken up the song. They sang about what a long way there was to go, and it seemed to Lila that those words meant a lot to them.

Then, suddenly, Grandmama squeezed her hand. "Look, Lila! Look who's waving!"

Lila turned. There on the curb were Mama and

Papa, and George in his carriage. Lila waved. Then the parade swept her on. She wondered whether Papa had noticed her stockings.

"Imagine your papa coming out for this parade!" Grandmama leaned over and hugged her. "You know, something tells me we're going to win! One of these days we'll be voting."

They marched on, past the reviewing stand. They marched until Lila's legs felt like stumps. They marched while the sun slid down in the sky and disappeared behind buildings.

It was twilight by the time the parade broke up and Grandmama said, "Let's go home in a cab." Lila was glad to hear that. She didn't feel like walking.

While they waited for a taxi, Lila looked down at her tomato-splattered stockings. She felt proud of them. They were like a badge. She didn't even think of rolling them down.

In 1848, Elizabeth Cady Stanton and Lucretia Mott met at Seneca Falls, New York, to draw up a declaration of women's rights. Now, the idea that women have rights is taken for granted. Then, it was not. Women had few rights and certainly not the right to vote. In their declaration, Mrs. Stanton and Mrs. Mott asked for that.

Both these women were abolitionists who worked before the Civil War for the freeing of slaves. Human rights included women's rights, they thought. If Negroes were freed and allowed to vote, couldn't women expect the same? It didn't work that way. After the Civil War, Congress passed the Fourteenth Amendment to the Constitution, permitting all citizens to vote, providing they were male! The women who had worked so hard for abolition were outraged.

In 1890, they formed the National American Woman Suffrage Association. Mrs. Stanton was its first president and working with her was another important woman in the suffrage movement, Susan B. Anthony. Together they were determined to win votes for women.

For the next thirty years, suffragists worked tirelessly. They collected signatures on petitions, traveled great distances to speak about suffrage, visited Congress and the president many times with their request. Over and over, they were turned down. Both President Woodrow Wilson and most members of Congress felt that women's suffrage was a matter to be decided by the individual states and not by a change in the Constitution. They were supported by numbers of men— and many women—who opposed women's right to vote at all. Finally, in frustration, the suffragists decided to begin picketing the White House.

This same year, 1917, the United States entered the First World War. American troops were sent to Europe to help England and France in their war with the Germans. Women's suffrage was not the main topic on the minds of the men in government. But the suffragists worked on.

In November, 1917, New York finally joined other states in granting women the right to vote. This was a turning point. Members of Congress began to see that pressure for a constitutional amendment was enormous. President Wilson gave it his support, and in 1919 the Senate voted in favor.

In August, 1920, the Nineteenth Amendment was finally ratified by two-thirds of the states, and after seventy years of trying, women had won the right to vote.

Z.O.